E DOR
Ricci, Christine.
I love my abuela! /

DORA the EXPLORER®
I Love My Abuela!

by Christine Ricci   illustrated by Victoria Miller

Simon Spotlight/Nickelodeon
New York   London   Toronto   Sydney

Based on the TV series *Dora the Explorer*® as seen on Nick Jr.®

SIMON SPOTLIGHT
An imprint of Simon & Schuster Children's Publishing Division
1230 Avenue of the Americas, New York, New York 10020
© 2009 Viacom International Inc. All rights reserved.
NICK JR., *Dora the Explorer*, and all related titles, logos, and characters are registered
trademarks of Viacom International Inc.
Manufactured in the United States of America
First Edition 10 9 8 7 6 5 4 3 2 1
ISBN-13: 978-1-4169-6866-5
ISBN-10: 1-4169-6866-0

¡Hola! I'm Dora. Do you know who this is? *¡Abuela!* My grandma! I love my *abuela*! *¡Quiero a mi abuela!*

Abuela and I are explorers! We both love to go hiking. She teaches me about the flowers and animals when we explore the mountains and meadows together.

I love to go hiking with *Abuela*! What do you like to do with your grandmother?

I'm a Star Catcher and so is *Abuela*! Did you know that *Abuela* gave me my Star Pocket and taught me how to catch stars?

I think some stars are hiding nearby. How many stars do you see? *¡Cinco!* Five!

Abuela and I can catch the five stars! We're both great Star Catchers!

What do you have in common with your grandmother?

Abuela can do so many things. She can swing on a vine!

She can jump over mud puddles and even climb a rock wall! My *abuela* is very strong and healthy! She helps me to be strong and healthy too!

Abuela shows me how to take good care of the plants and the trees. When *Abuela* was a little girl, she took care of our friend Chocolate Tree.

Do you like hot chocolate? It's my favorite drink. *Abuela* makes the best hot chocolate, and she's going to show me how to make it!

What delicious treat does your *abuela* make for you?

Do you like to dance? *Abuela* and I love to dance! When I visit *Abuela* after school, we turn on the radio and dance! *Abuela* showed me how to do the mambo and salsa. She even showed me how to twirl like a ballerina.

Whenever I learn a new dance, my *abuela* wants me to teach her how to do it! I love dancing with my *abuela*!

Abuela teaches me a lot about my family. Look at all the pictures of our family on her wall. Do you see the picture of me and *Abuela*?

Abuela lets me explore her attic and closet. She has the most beautiful clothes and jewelry. Which one is your favorite?

Abuela knows how to make me laugh! She makes the silliest faces. Even when I'm sad or upset, *mi abuela* can get me giggling!

Let's giggle together. Make a silly face like me!

Abuela loves to hear about my adventures, and I love it when she tells me stories about the adventures she went on when she was a little girl. One of my favorite things to do is to listen to *Abuela*'s stories. *Abuela* is the best storyteller.

Where do you like to go with your grandmother? I like it when *Abuela* takes me to the amusement park. We like the same rides. Our favorite ride is the roller coaster. Have you ever ridden a roller coaster?

Abuela tells me that when we get up to the top, I should put my hands in the air and say "Wheeeee!" If I get scared, she'll hold my hand. I like going on the rides with *Abuela*.

My *abuela* gives the best hugs. She wraps her arms around me and squeezes me, but not too tight. Then she gives me a big kiss. *Abuela*'s hugs make me feel so special! Do you like getting hugs from your grandmother?

Every day is an adventure with *Abuela*! There's always something exciting to discover when I'm with my grandma! I love my grandma! *¡Quiero a mi abuela!*